Dear Parent:
Your child's love of reading starts here!

Every child learns to read in a different way and at his or her own speed. You can help your young reader improve and become more confident by encouraging his or her own interests and abilities. You can also guide your child's spiritual development by reading stories with biblical values and Bible stories, like I Can Read! books published by Zonderkidz. From books your child reads with you to the first books he or she reads alone, there are I Can Read! books for every stage of reading:

 SHARED READING
Basic language, word repetition, and whimsical illustrations, ideal for sharing with your emergent reader.

BEGINNING READING
Short sentences, familiar words, and simple concepts for children eager to read on their own.

 READING WITH HELP
Engaging stories, longer sentences, and language play for developing readers.

 READING ALONE
Complex plots, challenging vocabulary, and high-interest topics for the independent reader.

 ADVANCED READING
Short paragraphs, chapters, and exciting themes for the perfect bridge to chapter books.

I Can Read! books have introduced children to the joy of reading since 1957. Featuring award-winning authors and illustrators and a fabulous cast of beloved characters, I Can Read! books set the standard for beginning readers.

A lifetime of discovery begins with the magical words **"I Can Read!"**

Visit www.icanread.com for information on enriching your child's reading experience.
Visit www.zonderkidz.com for more Zonderkidz I Can Read! titles.

"I have set my rainbow in the clouds."
— Genesis 9:13

ZONDERKIDZ

The Berenstain Bears®, God Made the Colors
Copyright© 2013 by Berenstain Publishing, Inc.
Illustrations © 2013 by Berenstain Publishing, Inc.

Requests for information should be addressed to:

Zondervan, 3900 *Sparks Drive SE, Grand Rapids, Michigan 49546*

Library of Congress Cataloging-in-Publication Data
Berenstain, Jan, 1923–2012.
        The Berenstain Bears : God made the colors / by Stan and Jan Berenstain
with Mike Berenstain.
               p.   cm. – (I can read! Level 1)
"Living Lights."
Summary: The Berenstain Bears love the colors in God's world, from a barn
painted red to the green found in nature to the different shades of people's
skins.
        ISBN 978-0-310-72507-7 (softcover)
        [1. Stories in rhyme. 2. Color– Fiction. 3. Bears–Fiction. 4. Christian life–
Fiction.] I. Berenstain, Mike, 1951– II. Title. III. Title: God made the colors.
        PZ8.3.B44925Bc   2013
        [E]–dc23   2012020267

Editor: Mary Hassinger
Design: Diane Mielke

Printed in China

15 16 17 18 19 20 • 10 9 8 7 6 5 4

The Berenstain Bears®
God Made
the Colors

Story and Pictures By
Stan & Jan Berenstain with Mike Berenstain

Living Lights™

We love colors—colors God made.

God made every single shade.

Red, red, we love red

like that barn painted bright barn red,

and that woodpecker's

bright red head.

Yellow, yellow!

We love yellow!

The color of the sun,

its brightest beam.

The yummy color

of lemon ice cream.

Do we love blue?

You bet we do!

The color of God's sky? Yes.

The color of Mama's

polka-dot dress.

But God made other colors too.

They come from mixing

yellow, red, and blue.

Mix red and yellow,

and what do you get?

Orange! Orange

is what you get.

God mixed colors and made them glow.

He made bright orange for nature's show.

The color of a leaf about to drop,

the color of a farmer's pumpkin crop.

The color of his carrot ...

of his hat ...

of his orange-colored cat.

Green is a super color too.

We get it by mixing

yellow and blue.

We love green. How about you?

It seems to be God's favorite too.

It's the color of nature all around,

of most things that grow

out of the ground.

Though all greens share
a single name,
all greens are not
the very same.

Some are dark.

Some are light.

Some are dull and

some are bright.

The fact, friends,
is also true
of all the other
colors too.

Colors, colors!

Dull and bright.

God made colors,

dark and light.

Wait! What about purple
which don't forget,
is also known as violet?

We get purple,
rich and fine,
when red and blue
we combine.

It is the color of grapes

on the vine.

The color of feet

that make grape wine.

We love yellow,

red, and blue.

We love green

and orange too.

And purple, of course,

which don't forget,

is also known as violet.

We see those colors

and lots more

at the paint

and hardware store.

Beige and tan,

buff and brown,

the colors of the bears

in our town.

God made bears and people too
of different color, different hue.

We love the color of every bear.

And the color of people everywhere.

God paints sunsets at the end of day.

At night the colors

all fade away.

It grows dark,

and darker still.

Will the colors come back?

Yes! Yes!

Yes, they will.

God makes the dawn of

another day.

The sun comes up.

Hooray! Hooray!

We get up, go out, and say …

God made the colors

red, yellow, and blue.

We love green

and orange too.

And purple, of course,

which don't forget,

is also called violet.